The Love of Marisol

Christos Toulouras

Wattle Publishing

Wattle Publishing Ltd
Third Floor, 207 Regent Street
London W1B 3HH
www.wattlepublishing.com

Published in Great Britain by Wattle Publishing Ltd in 2014

A catalogue record of this book is available from the British Library

ISBN 978-1-908959-25-6

First Published in 2010 by En Tipis Publications,
Chilis, 26, 1020 Pallouriotissa, Nicosia, Cyprus.

Printed and bound by CPI Group (UK) Ltd, Croydon, CR0 4YY

"Two men look through prison bars. One sees mud, the other stars."
Frederick Langbridge (1849-1923)

About the Author

Christos Toulouras was born in Cyprus. He has lived in South Africa and Cyprus. He studied Tourist administration in Thessaloniki. He continued his studies in the UK at Leicester University where he received his MBA. He currently lives in Cyprus.

Contents

One Night in Bahia

Leo saw the ceiling of the room descend so low that it almost touched the tip of his nose. However, he was not scared at all. He felt numb, weak, and so depressed that he had no desire to push the ceiling up to avoid the oncoming suffocation he was feeling. He chose to do what suited him at the time, to sink his slim body aimlessly into the middle of the mattress. All this time, his arms were crossed across his chest, and they felt very, very heavy. When he tried to lift his arms across the back of his head, the weight against his chest had not lifted but had remained intact. It was unbearable, like a cold slab of marble. He then realized that the weight he felt had nothing to do with his arms. He was constantly trying to take deep breaths; however, it was in vain! The oxygen could not reach his lungs; he desperately needed it. It would stop midway because his breath was so heavy. Each time he inhaled he felt as if his lungs would tear apart.

His gaze was fixated for a long time at a small crack on the ceiling; the crack ran along the surface, and he noticed that the cold surface was the color of magnolia. He reached his arm and with his thumb; he stroked the crack along its length, slowly, several times, as if he wanted to repair it.

He looked around the odorless room and had almost forgotten how he had gotten there. It was one of a dozen rooms in a small hotel near the airport, in Amsterdam. He had only been there for one day. He was planning to stay there for another day as he waited to catch a connecting flight to Lima, Peru to visit his cousins who lived there. He hoped that a short vacation might help him through this difficult time. He hoped that it would help to transform the blurring silent images in his head, which looked as if they came out of a battlefield massacre, to new ones, like a *Van Dyke* painting, with so much depth, bright colors and guitar sounds. He knew he needed this vacation to help him solve the bitter knot in his stomach. Since last week, especially after receiving the yellow document holder with the divorce papers he had finally hit rock bottom. Before the divorce, he had been separated from his wife for nine months – even so, it had not made the divorce any easier.

He had listened to his friends arguing that divorce papers were the passport to a temporary hell while others paralleled them to a million-dollar check. *Both these views are unrealistic* ... he thought as he drifted off to sleep.

The next morning he noticed that the ceiling was in no hurry to move from its fallen state, but he had to admit that he did not have the energy or the inclination to push it up. He was numb from sorrow and grieving. He preferred to lie in silence, staring aimlessly at the ceiling. The situation was stifling, mostly due to the lack of air and the confined space. During the night, Leo had woken up several times listening to his leaden breath, which was torturing his lungs, even in his sleep. He questioned whether he should go to Lima, or if he should return to his own country. He was not sure either way; both places seemed distant and indifferent.

His head was filled with images of his three-year-old son, his separation, and those divorce papers. Thoughts of his son often came to his mind. Although Leo had three short ephemeral affairs since his separation, his son, however, was all he could think of on his return home, after leaving these women. His son was his comfort to the melancholy these soulless affairs had brought.

After his son drifted from his thoughts, he reflected on his former wife. Even though he moved out of the house, he did not feel that he had lost his son. What tortured him was that he had lost his wife, with whom he had spent the last ten years of his life. She was his first love.

He recalled everything in just an hour. *Everything? This is such a misconception*! He thought *it was strange how you could recall images with such clarity.* It was like watching a film backwards; a long excerpt of his life and it came back so vividly that it haunted his very being. The human mind thinks that it can remember everything, but in reality, it only has a few recollections of the most intense experiences.

Some people think that they can reminisce about a whole relationship within an hour, half an hour or even a quarter of an hour. However, this is impossible. A whole lifetime of two people together cannot fit within a single recollection. People tend to remember only the good times and forget about the bad memories. After a break up, they dedicate their time to remembering the beautiful moments that they once shared. Like watching some melodramatic film, their memories only evoke tender moments of their marriage. They seem to forget how they got to this place. They forget the mundane moments, the tantrums, the vices that were spawned from meanness and mistakes. They seem to forget the cruelest of moments and when they were at their worse; threatening each other with cruel taunts "I could find someone better." They seem to forget how badly they talked to each other, how the words that were said cut deep and could change emotions, to destroy the happiness and replace it with pain, bitterness and anger. They seem to forget how they neglected to take care of this beautiful tree called 'marriage.'

For some reason, they seem to linger on the wonderful memories and somehow forget the cross words, the volatility and the craziness that comes from the disintegration of a couple who were once so madly, passionately in love, but had now fallen out of love and were no longer able to stay together. Some people choose to remember only the *good times* simply because they may not want to be overcome with emotional guilt with the realization that their actions caused the disintegration of their marriage. After a break up, some men selfishly think that their wife will soon sleep with another, and this sole thought enrages them. Some men don't even consider getting a divorce to avoid this, even if they cheated on their wives in the first place, and there is no passion or love within the marriage.

Leo shook his head as he thought that so many lack the courage and the conviction to give up on their relationships and get a divorce. He thought with sadness that so many of his fellow countrymen were stuck in loveless relationships. Some chose not to separate because of their children; even though they know in their hearts that they are no longer in love with each other. This was how children become unwitting scapegoats - the excuse.

His thoughts were making him feel weak and moody. His body sank deeper into the mattress as he lied there watching the melting ceiling above him. He looked at his watch and groaned inwardly. The sound of his watch reminded him that if he overslept, he would miss his flight and would have to spend another night in this room, as the next flight would not leave until the following day. The thought of having to spend another night in this tiny room further depressed him. He looked back up at the ceiling and shuddered as he recalled the previous night and the sadness he had felt. Without wasting another second and in order to avoid another miserable and lonely night, Leo picked himself up and slowly crawled off the bed. His body ached from the misery and with the weight of his depression sitting heavily on his shoulders; he got dressed, picked up his suitcase and left the room with a low ceiling.

Although Leo had visited many airports, he immediately noticed that this airport was by far the most modern that he had visited. It was bright, and there were striking colors everywhere. He noticed that there were so many shops and restaurants and even gaming halls. The building reminded him of a shopping mall rather than an airport. He followed the signs and went up to the first floor. Thankfully, he had chosen to wear his dark-blue tracksuit rather than trousers. He had correctly thought *that he would feel more comfortable in these clothes during the fourteen-hour flight.*

He looked around and found that the benches were filled with the transatlantic airline staff waiting to board their flights. He noticed that there were swarms of beautiful, young and well-groomed women who were smiling jovially. They all had their hair coiffed in an array of styles. People were talking loudly with the blur of noise interrupted by the stream of announcements that were being broadcasted over the public addressing system in a variety of different languages. Here, in contrast with the ground floor, everything reminded Leo of how an airport should look; he stood in a long line and waited his turn to check his suitcase and receive his boarding pass. Standing in front of him was a young couple that displayed their affection by passionately kissing. The young man had long, unruly hair, a scraggly beard and was dressed like a hippy. He looked unwashed. He had a black guitar case that hung loosely on his back. The girl was much shorter but dressed in the same style as her partner. Even though they were traveling together, they kissed each other passionately and longingly as if they were saying good-bye, as if each kiss was to be their last. The girl clung so tightly to her boyfriend; it was as if she feared that he might reconsider and leave her behind!

As Leo watched the couple, he thought of a discussion he had with his brother the year before, when Leo had visited him in England. He recalled with distinct clarity the rainy afternoon when his brother picked him up from the airport. During their two-hour drive to his brother's home, they spoke in general terms about *relationships*. His brother said something he remembered because it had struck a nerve. "There is one thing that can tell you more about a troubled relationship than anything else; the kiss. As things start to turn bad, it gradually disappears and eventually is inexistent within the relationship. Not even during lovemaking. And neither one of the partners realizes what is happening when kissing starts to disappear from the relationship and instead of trying to bring it back and rekindle the spark in the relationship. It is like 'The End' on the screen at the movies. According to the film critic Michael Althen, it is no longer used anymore but nobody can remember when it was completely removed from the movies."

Leo was in a trance as he recalled the conversation, completely unaware of what was happening around him. A ground crew official interrupted his thoughts by lightly tapping him on the shoulder and asked, "Sir, where are you traveling to?"

"Sorry, I did not hear you." Leo replied. He walked towards the counter, where the clerk smiled openly at him and asked.

"Where are you traveling Sir?"

"To Lima."

Leo noticed how strikingly beautiful the counter clerk was as she smiled warmly and replied, "Sir, you have queued at the wrong counter." Pointing towards another counter and added, "You should go to that line." He turned, looking at the line and groaned inwardly realizing that he had wasted so much time. He picked up his bags and walked over.

The plane to Lima was over-crowded, and as it started to depart the noise from the propellers was so loud that it deafened Leo's eardrums. He was slightly annoyed at not being able to 'listen' to his thoughts and wished that the noise would subside. The noise carried with it such intensity that it affected him to his core; his ears were humming from the sound, and his head was throbbing from the noise. Leo looked around and noticed that most of the passengers appeared to be South Americans returning from Europe back to their homeland, interspersed with European tourists who were excitedly reading their Peru guidebooks. He wondered if some of the passengers were like him – desperately searching for something new, although he was still unclear as to why he had chosen to make such a long and arduous journey.

The fourteen-hour flight was long and at times an uncomfortable journey, mainly because of his feelings of loneliness and fear. He felt the same claustrophobia that he had expressed the night before in his tiny, dark hotel room. He kept looking at his watch anxiously, trying to calculate the time of his journey and arrival to Lima bearing in mind the time difference. Suddenly, he felt relieved because he remembered that he had brought a book that he had long waited to read with him on this trip. He took it out from his carryall and began to read it. He immediately became engrossed in the characters, setting and descriptive language of the author. He thought it was a wonderful story. After a few hours, he fell asleep.

Suddenly, Leo woke up abruptly. The weight in his chest that had burdened him the previous night had returned, engulfing his every pore and overcoming him, feelings of grief, emptiness and sorrow. He ate some food and reflected on his former wife and soon realized he could not shake her from his mind.

Eventually, he tried to ignore these thoughts by gazing at his fellow passengers in the hope of trying to keep his mind busy; he drank beer and wine and tried to relax. Finally, he began to relax. The burden that he had that he had felt within him though, would not shift, and he solemnly realized that regardless of how much alcohol he consumed that this sadness; this terrible pit in his stomach, and the burden in his chest would not go away.

The noise of the jets which had initially tormented him and his thoughts, no longer seemed so unbearable. Perhaps it was because he had got use to the sound over the course of the flight. "Everything becomes a habit" his cousin Dom had once told him. Dom also got a divorce the previous year. Leo remembered them sitting by the sea one barmy September a few years ago talking with an open candor about relationships.

"Ultimately cousin, when two people are about to separate, they initially cling to each other as they are sad to let go, and they may regret their decision, so they want to go back; perhaps it is a habit, maybe regret. Habit has so much power that it can even make a cheating spouse not want a divorce. Habit can even cause the man who lived in a prison cell for twenty years not want to leave. Sometimes, people are so weak that they are frightened to leave an unhealthy relationship because they are afraid to let go. Is it a habit? Or is it the fear of having to sail into the unknown? The unfamiliar may also cause people to feel enormous fear and uncertainty."

Leo tried to escape his dreary and sad thoughts by thinking of something else. He wondered what language was spoken in Peru and assumed that it was Spanish; a language which he had always liked. He was then distracted by the conversation of two Italians who were seated near him. They were speaking very loudly. Leo wondered if people spoke Italian in Peru. Leo spoke Italian very well, having some time ago lived *in the country that was shaped like a boot*. He liked to travel, and he especially liked countries where he was charmed by the language such as Spain, Italy and England.

He approached the Italians who were standing in the plane's aisle and greeted them. He realized that he desperately wanted to talk to someone, having been isolated and alone for almost two days. He wanted to say something, but at the same time he realized that he was unable to conjure up the words and describe what he was feeling. He was also sure that they would not be interested in listening to him talk about his pain. Although he realized that what was happening to him was not the end of the world and that countless others were experiencing similar depths of loss from the end of their marriage, it didn't help ease his pain. He felt lonely and heartbroken. He realized that he was only in his thirties and that, in the future, he could well meet someone else. However for now at least, he was swamped with feelings of sadness and remorse that were caused entirely by the loss and anxiety of his separation. He wanted desperately to speak with someone and rationalize his thinking, but he wasn't sure that he was ready or if anyone wanted to listen to his story.

Eventually, Leo started to make polite chit chat with the Italians. They assured him that Spanish was very similar to Italian. Tonino was from Calabria and Michele from Turin. Michele worked for a company that specialized in exporting chocolates to Peru and was traveling there on a business trip. Leo noticed that he was somewhat bored. Tonino looked more cheerful, and explained to Leo how easy it was to learn Spanish. Leo tried to focus on the conversation just to simply engage with another human being; to forget his woes and the divorce that only a few days prior eclipsed his entire thoughts and being.

"What are you going to do in Peru?" Tonino asked with great interest. "I am visiting my cousins," Leo replied. He was ashamed to say that, in reality, he did not want to visit or see anyone. *Who would believe that he would take a fourteen-hour flight to go to the other side of the world without wanting to see anyone?*

"What are you going to do in Peru?" Leo asked, more out of politeness than genuine interest. "I'm going to marry the girl of my dreams," Tonino replied with bravado. Leo was surprised by his reply. The Italian sensing Leo's reaction continued "It is a girl that I met on the Internet."

Leo looked at him with a stone-cold expression. *What an idiot* he thought to himself. *Could he not find a woman in Italy? He learned to speak Spanish for a woman on the other side of the world, who he had only met via the Internet and was intending to marry her even though he had never met her before.* Leo thought *that he was either a hopeless romantic or a complete fantasist.* Tonino spoke with confidence about his trip to Peru and his marital plans. He looked like a very enthusiastic guy who had just fallen in love and had the best intentions towards his partner and future wife. Or was it that he had fallen in love with the idea of love? Leo couldn't believe that he was going to spend the rest of his life with a woman whom he had at no time seen in person, someone whom he had never kissed or touched or shared intimacy with.

"Life is a little crazy," said Leo out loud. Even so, he quickly recalled his own predicament and became quiet. He looked at Tonino's face and found that his skin glowed despite the hours they had been traveling. He wondered if Tonino really knew what he was getting himself into. He certainly seemed ready to lay the milestones to his marriage. *Was it just the excitement of the unknown though?*

Leo thought that the "Wedding Tower" was similar to the "Tower of Babel." In order for a tower to be built well, it not only needs a good foundation but every day, every stone needs to be properly attended to and put into place. Leo had *first-hand experience.* He smiled wryly, thinking about his Tower that had fallen and now lay in ruins, and Leo became introspective. The tower that he and his wife had founded was built on imperfection and did not have the solid foundations that it required to withstand the test of time. It had been built with defects that had become increasingly exposed over time. How was he going to survive in the ruins?

With a wry smile, he politely left the two Italians and went back to his seat. What he had wanted to say, he did not feel would have been well-received by Tonino. And Michele was focused on his business and did not to be in the mood to discuss anything apart from work. He wanted to caution them both; he remembered what it was like to be in love. However, he thought better of it; the last thing you want to hear from someone was negative comments - especially from someone who had just separated. Besides, if Tonino wished to continue his quest to meet his future wife in Peru, who was Leo to jeopardize his romantic notions?

They had only been traveling for six hours; he looked around to find that most of the passengers were sleeping dreamily. There were still another eight hours to go and for Leo this seemed like forever. He closed his eyes but could not fall asleep. He looked around the cabin desperately wanting conversation but realized that he did not want to speak to the Italians again. He looked across at the people seating next to him; they were an Indigenous family from Peru. At the beginning of the trip, he had tried to talk with them, but they had failed to communicate, with each other. He leaned his head against the small airline pillow and tried to relax. He recalled his conversation with Tonino. Leo wondered at how sure this man was about his intentions. He thought it strange how he seemed so full of confidence and bravado about the success of this relationship to a total stranger. Leo remembered that he had never been so openly confident of marriage. He remembered that he was simply in love when he proposed. *I wonder;* he thought, *if I were a more positive thinker, and had based more of my actions on love, whether my marriage would have survived, and I wouldn't have lost Rafaela.*

He was only twenty years of age when he got married. He now realized that he wasn't mature enough to settle down at such a very young age. He thought that he had read somewhere that scientists claimed the brain of a man does not fully form until they are twenty-five. How can a 'child' think clearly and make such life-changing decisions?

Maybe it was his immaturity that had contributed to the disintegration of their relationship.

Leo began to consider the things that may have averted the inevitable. Was it a lack of tenderness when he made love to her? Was it that he always forgot to buy several items from the shopping list? Was it that he did not compromise often enough? Was he, the main culprit and the one to blame? He started to feel weary, and his body began to shake from the sorrow. He was full of remorse and guilt about the disintegration of the relationship.

He remembered with clarity one afternoon in late May when he went to visit his ex-wife. He asked her to give their relationship another chance. It was a hot afternoon, so they sat on the balcony. Leo had hoped that she would say that she still loved him and that they could be a family again. More so, when he looked deep into Rafaela's eyes as he spoke, he finally realized how she really felt, even before she answered. As he spoke, her face had already changed. She went from being the sweetest person Leo knew to an aggressive woman who he hardly recognized. She seemed to have forever lost her innocence. She stood up, and full of anger and pain, pushed him out of the house. *She treated me so horribly!* Leo thought. *She was acting like a wild woman, consumed with rage.* He tried to visit her a week later, and she asked him for the house keys. At the time, he still thought that she was overacting and that she was consumed with unreasonable rage. He was not sure how they had ended up in this place. Leo was devastated. He then remembered discussing this incident with his aunt who told him "So she kicked you out, and you are still thinking of her? What an idiot, you are!" How right, was his aunt after all!

During his flight to Lima, Leo could not realize this simple truth, nor was he ready to understand what happened. However, he would realize everything a year later following his trip to Peru. Up until then he could not accept that the love between, he and Rafaela was gone forever and, like millions of other couples in this world. Their relationship had finished even before they divorced. Their separation had begun when they had started to sit in silence on the couch before silently moving to bed, as if they were ignoring each other's presence. And even sadder, when they made love there was no emotion, no spark … they were already separated.

He stared around the cabin and realized that he felt frustrated, as he did not know how to pass the time. He did not have anyone to speak with and share his woes. At that moment, while flying over the Gulf of Mexico, he decided to write. He called the air stewardess over and asked for a pen and a notebook.

In my life, I have met many different types of people. At some point, many of these people have made wrong choices and have suffered for a long time, some even for the rest of their lives. Some people get divorced because they married young, and the only criteria for their marriage were the erotic passion that existed and initially bound them together while they had nothing else in common. The match was spawned from carnage desire in contrast to the friendship and communication that is needed between two people. The only thing that Rafaela and I had in common was that we supported the same football team because we were born in the same town. Communication did not exist between us. I now realize that I was once blinded by the passion and the eroticism that existed in our sex life and that the love that we shared was based upon passion alone. It did not provide a proper foundation, and as we grew older, our differences became increasingly apparent, worsened by the fact that there was no appetite for compromise. When two people in a relationship cannot communicate, when the first sign of difficulty erupts, its tremors affect the 'Tower of Marriage' and as the tremors keep occurring overtime given the poor foundation of the relationship, the tower eventually collapses. Some relationships will collapse straight away while others become derelict over time as was our case.

"Why do people get married?" Leo wondered to himself and twisted uncomfortably in his seat. He continued to write, *What is it that makes a man afraid of the sanctity and commitment required by marriage?* He noted that some feared the pressures of succumbing to women in general. Some women he knew used their charms to get men to buy them expensive rings, flowers, spend money on glamorous and expensive restaurants to impress and guarantee the marriage proposal.

But then what happens? Leo reflected on his partnership and continued to write, *Everyone carries personal, everyday habits, how we eat, how we perform our household duties like folding clothes - things that we pick up as we grow up. Very soon, the passion and the love begins to dither away, and couples start to fight over the most mundane and trivial of things; the constant sniping and degradation become unbearable. Couples fight more and more about how untidy the man is or how unstylish the woman has become. They keep complaining about small and insignificant things like when one forgets to bring something from the supermarket or fails to refill the car with petrol. Eventually, these differences shake the foundation of the relationship until they arrive at a point where they no longer have common ground; the "Tower of Marriage" disintegrates as the couple is no longer on the same page, looking in the same direction.*

As Leo wrote these thoughts on his notepad, he recalled other moments from his failed relationship. After some time, he dozed off to sleep. However, it was not relaxing, refreshing sleep because he woke up with a heavy head, and his legs were slightly swollen. *Flights are always like this;* he thought. A few moments later the air stewardess announced in a very bad English accent that they were due to arrive in Lima. Although Leo was not sitting near the window, he could still see a hazy sky and under it, an ocean of lights and buildings. Lima: A city that he had only ever heard about maybe two or three times before in his life.

The Smell of Lima

The plane finally touched down. Leo was exhausted. He had been traveling for a total of fifteen hours with just one stop. During the time, he had been seated, he had been desperate to stretch his legs, walk around and feel human again. He waited for what seemed like an eternity to collect his blue suitcase from the conveyor belt, and as he left the baggage hall and opened his hand luggage, he searched for his red address book. His cousins' contact details were inside; Dom and Pita. However, he was confident that at least one of his cousins would already be there waiting to meet him. Leo's cousins were born and raised in Peru. They owned an upmarket restaurant near the beach. They cooked delicious and inspired cuisine; meat was their speciality.

Their customers were rich and enjoyed the fine-dining experience. Both his cousins were accomplished chefs. Their father and Leo's uncle, many years ago immigrated to Peru by boat, along with a dozen other villagers. His relatives had worked very hard and toiled in this new land, and some of them had amassed great wealth. However, whilst some of the immigrants succeeded others had not. The ones that were not able to amass a small fortune found themselves returning to the village.

Leo's uncle had held a number of jobs until he had saved enough money to open a jewelry store. He worked extremely hard with his wife, Adele. One day, she left him for a blue-eyed Russian naval officer, this crushed his uncle who eventually decided to hire a manager and leave the shop. He then languished. He did nothing but drink as he was consumed with grief and betrayal, feeling that his honor had been destroyed. He was consumed, to a degree; that was unspeakable and for a period of thirteen years he refused to venture out. When he died, he left his sons the jewelry store. They sold it and opened a restaurant near the beach. It had been almost two years since he had seen last Dom and Pita. The last time he saw them was at a family wedding. Nevertheless, he had spent many summer holidays with his cousins when they were younger because their father often sent them back to the village on holidays. So despite his sorrow and sadness, he welcomed the opportunity to see his cousins and to renew the special bond that had formed between them over the years.

The last time Leo saw Dom, he was kind of chubby with a long, blond ponytail, down to his waist. With this image in his head, he was trying to recognize his cousin from the rest of the people waiting at the Arrivals Hall. However, he was not there.

While he waited at the Arrivals Hall, he was amazed by the smell that lingered in the air. It was something he was unfamiliar with. It gave Leo a peculiar sensation of love and danger. He didn't even know if Lima was a dangerous city. To his right, he noticed that someone was loitering behind the parked buses. Rather than realizing that intrigue was rife, he thought of this man as the God of Love, who was responsible for the strange scent in the air, gaining its mysterious, dangerous edge. He was real, but to Leo, he looked, he could have come out of a Renaissance painting. However, Lima's God of Love was slimmer, and his bow thicker, so that it wouldn't break while shooting off so many arrows.

Leo realized that he had seen the God of Love before, in Greece and Italy, where he had previously lived for a few years, but the allure of Lima's God of Love was different. It was mixed with a scent that felt strangely attractive and at the same time *dangerous*. There were different rules that accompanied each city. The scent of Lima would remain with him forever in his consciousness. For as long as, he lived he would recall that aroma. The memories from this time would be etched heavily in Leo's memory. He would often recall the trip whilst listening to vibrant music or looking at the photographs he had taken there, which were filled with hope and sensuality. Whenever he ate mangoes, he would smell Lima's scent again being reminded of the place where he tried his first mango. Only two words could describe it: love and danger.

Leo started feeling more concerned that he did not see his cousins anywhere. The local taxi drivers approached him and tried to barter a fare, but he declined their offer. More so, they kept coming back in the hope that he would reconsider. They were closing in on him like vultures that could smell their prey. He pulled out his book and began to read to try to divert their attention in the hope of them leaving him alone. But, they just became increasingly aggressive in trying to get his business as the number of passengers left dwindled away.

A few more minutes passed and suddenly, amidst the noise around him. Leo heard a familiar voice from behind. "Hello cousin, come here!" He turned and saw a slim looking Dom without his blonde plait walking quickly towards him. Dom embraced him in a hurry and said "I have parked the car in the underground parking," making hand gestures as he spoke. "How do you feel? How was the trip?" Strangely, Dom seemed nervous while his simple questions to the jet lagged Leo, who was unclear how to respond to them. He wanted to share his news, but he also felt exhausted.

"We need to stop by the restaurant and pick up some things before we head home. We won't be too long. When we get home, you can shower before we go out for dinner and then head out to the local nightclubs afterwards." Dom eagerly said. Turning for a split second as he drove, he winked at Leo and added "only the best of Lima for you. We have the most beautiful women in this country." Even though Leo felt exhausted after almost two days of travel, he did not have the energy to protest his cousin's generosity.

Leo stared out the window and realized that he felt tired and that his heart still ached from the problems that he had experienced. The toil of the long flight, the uncomfortable hotel and the longing that he felt just compounded his misery. He also felt dehydrated and realizing that he had not even changed the time on his watch.

During the car trip, he was pleased to be with his cousin, even though he quizzed him constantly about his divorce. Dom had heard about Leo's separation six months ago and was under the impression that his cousin would have already left it behind. When he realized that Leo was not over it, he turned to his cousin and tried to encourage him to remain upbeat.

"You must forget her now! You are in Peru. There are many beautiful women here, and you are single!"

Leo reluctantly nodded, raised his head and looked out the window – the scene that lay in front of him was disconcerting. The streets were filthy and downtrodden, and some of the sidewalks were full of rubbish. Leo thought it looked completely improvised.

As they drove down some narrow alleys, he noticed food stalls lined up that sold different kinds of food. He saw people with dark clothes that looked more like shadows than actual people; eating and talking to each other. Almost all the walls were adorned with colorful graffiti. There were large letters that Leo assumed were politically linked. He noticed that, in every building, a national flag was displayed. They ranged in all sizes, and occasionally they moved slightly in the gentle breeze. Looking outside the window, Leo asked his cousin, "Why are there so many flags everywhere, Dom?" Without looking back, he replied "It is mid-July, and we are preparing for the national celebration towards the end of the month. The law requires all homes in Peru to display the national flag" replied Dom matter-of-factly.

They passed darker, dustier roads, and Leo thought *what a downtrodden country. Why did I come here? It is like another planet ...* Suddenly his thoughts were interrupted as the car came to an abrupt stop, and Leo realized that they had arrived at his cousins' restaurant, which was called 'Taurus.' The two cousins got out of the car and walked into the restaurant. It was a small restaurant on

Larco promenade parallel to the beach. Upon entering the restaurant, Leo noticed it had an open grill on the right where the cooks roasted meat in front of their customers. There was a small but well-stocked and stylish bar. There were lots of art works displayed in the restaurant. They were colorful paintings of bullfights and other local images. The restaurant was full to the brim. Most of the patrons were middle-aged couples and small groups. The smell of meat being grilled and roasted filled the restaurant. Ordinarily, Leo would have loved the smells of the restaurant, however; he was still getting use to his surroundings, and he felt somewhat dizzy from his flight.

Noticing Leo looking at the paintings, Dom asked, "Did you know that we have some very famous bullfights cousin?" "It actually started here were upon some Spaniards took it back to their country." Dom added. Although Leo was not convinced that the origins of bullfighting started in Peru, he chose to smile at his cousin rather than argue.

A well-dressed middle-aged gentleman came up to his cousin and greeted him warmly. He was dressed in a grey suit and wore glasses. The man was introduced to Leo as the manager of the restaurant; Alvaro was his name. A beautiful blonde girl was standing beside him. Her name was Erasmia. She was a waitress, and her marvelous beauty confirmed Leo's belief that the most beautiful women were not seen in fashion magazines and TV. He was convinced that some of the most beautiful women he had met worked in the most ordinary of establishments, such as restaurants, supermarkets, as sales assistants, or worked in kiosks, bakeries and factories. Erasmia was extremely attractive and definitely fitted this category. She had a beautiful, wide smile and was very pleasant.

Alvaro discreetly said something to Dom, and then they both looked at Leo from the corner of their eyes. Leo wondered what was being said but he was too polite to ask. Dom then explained that Alvaro was asking if they were heading out for drinks later or if Leo was tired and preferred to sleep, laughing that he may not be up for a night of drinking and dancing. Leo reassured him that he would be okay. He then joked, adding that all he needed a shot of caffeine to regain his stamina.

"Let's eat first," Dom said. "We will take you to La Gloria. It is a wonderful restaurant. We would prefer, dear cousin, to eat something different. We get slightly tired of eating beef every day. Tonight we will dine out to celebrate your arrival! Tomorrow we can eat here. Pita is also coming back from Brazil. You remember him don't you? You have met him before." Dom smiled.

Leo felt less sad and did not feel the weight in his chest as intensely as before. With all the people around him, there were moments where he forgot about the hurt and pain of losing his wife. They left the restaurant and walked back to the car. Leo was in a hazy dream. He felt slightly disorientated, as if he had lost all sense of time.

After looking at his watch, he realized that he would have been seen getting up to go to work if he were still in Europe. But here, now in Lima, he was planning to go to his Dom's house, shower, change and head out for a night of entertainment with his cousin. However, Leo did not have the heart to tell his cousin that he would have preferred to stay home and wallow in his sorrow. Staring out of the window once again, Leo found that he was tired, but it wasn't just because of his trip. He felt weary and challenged by the months that had led up to his separation.

During the car ride back to the house, the dizziness kept growing, which was not helped by the winding roads and array of unrecognizable smells to try and feel better. Leo fully unwound his window and pushed out his head to feel the air on his face. As cars passed them on the highly congested roads, female eyes stared at Dom's car and directly at them. Some of the glares were erotic, others sexy and some were simply funny. Leo felt overwhelmed by the intensity of the stares. He wasn't sure if he enjoyed the attention, or if he felt uncomfortable.

As Leo sat back into his seat, Dom announced, "this weekend we will head to Playa Blanca, the White Beach. We have rented a house there for the summer with the rest of the gang; Zamora, Kily, Kobe and Herman. We will have an amazing time!" Leo thought *that this sounded like a wonderful way to spend the weekend*. He had forgotten what it was like to enjoy his life and live in the moment.

Following the birth of his son, there was little opportunity to go out on guys' nights. All of his outings were with his wife. They would usually head for a coffee or to dinner, but they were always back by 11 pm, as if they were an old couple that had to get to sleep early.

"You know something Dom. Hanging out with other guys can be the most successful psychotherapy. This is when men talk, laugh, have fun and become open with each other. After I had separated, I realized that I lost many of my friends during my marriage, without even realizing it. I had forgotten the importance of my friendship, and I thought it was normal to live entirely through my wife, to the point that my only friend was my wife – what a mistake that was! I should have worked harder to retain my friendships. I realize that now! Many young men like me fall in love helplessly and devote their entire life to making their partner happy and spending time with her. For some reason, most men are unable to manage their lives and keep some part of their old selves. Of course, it doesn't help if your wife doesn't like your friends. In my situation, it started off with little remarks about not spending enough time together, and eventually I thought that the nagging and constant complaints were not worth the hassle. So I sacrificed the relationships that were once so important to me, because I was trying to keep the peace with my partner. I became embarrassed at neglecting my friends and realized that many friendships were severed. Further, my new friends became friends we met as a couple, and I never had the time I needed to do my own thing with my own friends.

"I will never allow such a thing to happen again ever!" Dom finished in earnest. Leo was silent for a moment and then looked out the window and said while gazing the road. "Those were my exact words before Rafaela ..."

Nena

They passed through some more disturbing, miserable and poor looking neighborhoods on the way back to Dom's apartment. Leo asked his cousin the names of each of the areas as they passed them. San Miguel, Magdalena Del Mar and Sourko. Each of the names sounded exotic to Leo and so different to those from where he was from. There was an aura of poverty and misery that he was still not accustomed to – he couldn't help but feel the sadness towards the poverty that he saw.

Many of the districts that they passed were the same. Most of the buildings were low rise and there were very few tall buildings. Many of the buildings appeared disheveled in need of urgent refurbishment. However, it was not only the buildings that required a facelift. Many of the roads, sidewalks, and small courtyards all looked like they had seen better days.

Gradually, the streets improved as they drew nearer to Dom's house, and the neighborhoods started to look a little better as they approached the main promenade along the sea. To the right, beneath the hill were the sea and a small park. Although it was evening, Leo could still see the beautiful plants and flowers that framed near the ocean beyond. To the left, there were new apartment blocks with modern styled entrances and set in beautiful gardens. There were security guards everywhere patrolling the buildings. Dom pulled up in front of these buildings and switched off the engine. They finally arrived!

"What is this neighborhood called?" Leo asked his cousin.

"Barranko, it means canyon." Leo whispered "Barranko" and tilted his head backwards in awe of his surroundings. Even though he was exhausted, his new surroundings lifted his spirit. Leo thought to himself – it was strange how we first hear the word and identify with this word; be it either place or person, how that word follows us throughout our lives – and may have the ability to change our lives. A simple word can awaken our senses and memories. And all this just from the sound of a simple word, which can unlock our minds to reveal an endless world of memories.

They walked towards Dom's building and entered the apartment. Leo was relieved to be safely indoors. His cousin offered him a beer, but Leo asked for coffee. He hoped that the caffeine would give him the necessary boost to make it through the night without collapsing. Leo quickly drank his coffee then looked at his cousin.

"I'll jump into the shower now and promise to be quick. "Leo's voice sounded a haggard and jaded. Dom realized that his cousin had been through a lot over the last couple of months and especially over the last few days and stared at his cousin compassionately.

"Try not to fall asleep in the shower! I'm sure that you will get into the rhythm of Lima's climate in no time."

Leo said nothing. He got up and walked towards the bathroom. He turned on the hot water. As the surge of water spluttered through the shower head, tears formed in his eyes. Leo felt like a child with no sense of control. He needed to be held, but he was all alone. He felt hopeless and sorry for himself. He realized that he was lonely in this distant country, and even though he was with relatives, he felt an intense inner solitude.

Leo thought of his father. He was a man who was incapable of offering any emotional comfort. His father considered emotional problems as a sign of weakness and emotions in general to be second-rate life experiences. He thought of his mother, who in stark contrast was quite romantic in her youth according to Leo's aunt. She had started off as a carefree spirit and enjoyed regular rendezvous to the seaside. However, by the time Leo was old enough to engage with his mother on such issues of the heart, she had regressed and had never shared her experiences or views about relationships with her son. Leo realized that his mother was like so many other women who had only found perfect love in their youth. Over time, this love had dissipated, as the passion that she once shared by his father in their youth faded. Leo realized that his mother had forgotten what it was like to be in love and to share this with him. So for as long as Leo could remember, he had never spoken with his parents about relationships, although admittedly, he did not even feel entirely comfortable discussing his relationships with his parents.

Leo was all alone, and he did not even have a friend who could offer any advice or advise him more meaningful than the usual glib mock comments like "Forget about her," or "it's her loss!" He felt very lonely when he was rejected by his previous loves. With each separation, he felt as helpless as a castaway in wild water, even if he was to blame for the failure of the relationship, or the one who decided the break up. When the only advice a young man gets is that he would find another woman soon, or that being rejected was to be expected, how could he possibly understand the opposite sex, to understand what went wrong and not make the same mistakes again. The repetition of such a cycle happens after enough time that you finally end up thinking that his is normal. Now in his thirties, Leo could recall having only even fallen in love twice before he met Rafaela. Sure, he spent some time flirting and chasing other women. However, he had only ever fallen in love twice.

Suddenly he heard a loud thud at the bathroom door. "Cousin, do you need a towel? Are you okay?" Dom asked.

"I'm fine" replied Leo.

Dom found Leo combing his hair. He saw that his cousin's eyes were red when he saw his face reflected in the mirror and realized that he must have been weeping in the shower. Dom stood in front of him and sighed.

"I get it that you feel like you have been punched in the stomach because of the divorce. However, you need to be strong. You will find in time that things will improve that life will go on, and everything will go back to normal just like it always does for everyone who goes through this."

"Normal?" Leo laughed nervously.

He had just faced his greatest challenge. He had separated from a woman whom he had fallen in love with at a very young age. The only other time he had felt this depressed was when he was fourteen-years-old student and was rejected by a fifteen-year-old girl named Avva. Even though another girl, Sophia was head over heels for him, he only wanted Avva. Men always seek the unattainable. Men are simple creatures; they want to *win,* and somehow their egos are bruised in the process. This may have been part of the problem. Leo wondered if perhaps very little changed in the soul of a rejected teen to the soul of a rejected man in his thirties.

The worst part of the separation for Leo was when it came to his son. Rafaela was still a young, vibrant and attractive woman. At some point, he knew she would meet someone, a stranger. They would start dating and eventually; he would move in. Leo feared being replaced as the new man would spend more time with his son than Leo was legally entitled to under the settlement. This is the worst part of the separation, especially given how young his son was; that this new man could end up being viewed by his child as a father figure and not him. Leo thinking about these fears gave Dom a grave and troubled look and signed:

"One day, when you have children of your own, you will understand it is not so simple. You will be one of us and realize the impact that they have on your life. A parent's love for their child is unconditional – remember the way we were loved as children?"

When Leo walked out of the bathroom, he felt a combination of cold sweat and sadness merging together. He felt strangely numb, and he could still feel that the burden on his chest. Depression and sadness hit people differently and to different degrees. For some people, grief lasts just for a few hours or a few weeks; for others; it may last longer, even forever. Leo felt convinced that the only people who did not have a place in their heart for such sadness, were those who were single. They were still emotional and therefore could not be afraid of what's around them. They could not be affected by what they could not see or hear. Leo envied them. They were the lucky ones who had the courage to go out in the light, dive into the sea and bathe in the midday sun and under the moonlight. They preferred sunlight from shadow, summer and spring from winter, feelings from illusions, and horses from bikes, the small and important gestures than big and pointless. Leo was at rock bottom.

And with this burden within his chest, Leo left the house with Dom.

Dom drove for some distance until they reached an apartment block in the same district. It was quite old, with the weedy sidewalks. "We have arrived at my friend Kobe's house. He is a great guy, slightly crazy - but great! You will see!" Leo considered that Kobe *had* to be a great guy as men generally considered that the 'crazier' their friends were the better.

Kobe, despite being tall and skinny, looked like a "tough guy" with thick black short hair and big green eyes. He was well dressed in that tough guy sort of way. He seemed pleased to meet Leo. He started talking really fast! This made a great first impression on Leo, who was always suspicious of the silent types.

They sat on the balcony where a cooling breeze was blowing in from the Pacific Ocean. Kobe offered Leo an

'Inca Kola' soft drink and explained that it was a very popular drink and sold everywhere. He began to tell Leo how he was originally from Canada and why he moved to Peru. Leo found Kobe to be funny and a great story teller. Kobe worked for a company selling restaurant equipment. He had studied at a university in California for five years before moving there.

"Originally, I come here as a nostalgic grungy hippie during the early nineties on holiday with my friends from university. I found the place very exotic, and I decided that I would return one day. When I went back to Canada, despite it being the place where I was born and had spent most of my life, I decided to sell my car and took the little money that I had saved and moved to Peru without any reservations.

I first went to Punta Hermosa where for a short period of time, I worked in an open bar on the beach. It was a great spot where all kinds of tourists would gather. I made a small but decent living. I lived like this for almost a year. During that time, I met a sexy and crazy English girl who ran a travel shop. We had a wonderful time together, and I have so many fond memories. We would eat fish at a nearby tavern drinking dark beer or Pisco. We would then return to the beach or simply laze around and smoke marijuana. At the end of each month, I would run out of money. I realized that even if I had wanted to return home, I couldn't afford the ticket.

The Marijuana had really affected my mind, and stopped me from seeing things clearly by creating a world of illusions. For example, I was convinced that I had made so many close friends from the bar's regulars whom I mistakenly thought if I asked someone they would lend me money to return to Canada. Believing this meant that I never bothered to change my lifestyle. For a time, the delusions that lay to rest any uncertainty or concerns that I had. However, the insecurities brought by this way of living eventually almost destroyed me; both physically and psychologically."

"Tell us more!" Leo said intrigued at Kobe's story.

"After a year a guy named Neil came to the bar. He was quite weird if I am being honest. He was also a Canadian from Montreal. He had lived in Lima for many years and was an entrepreneur in the restaurant equipment industry. Over the course of the week, Neil would be in the bar at noon, so we would eat together and talk about his work. I quickly realized that I was wasting my time working in a bar and struggling to make ends meet month to month. I was living beyond my means, and I suddenly came to the realization that I wanted more out of life. One day, Neil asked me where I saw myself in ten years, and I replied with candor "nowhere, anywhere."

He offered me a job in Lima because he needed a Canadian to work with him. In the end, I didn't even think twice; I left the bar, cut my long hair and burned my clothes on the beach. I then picked up my backpack, put it across my shoulder and said good-bye to my girlfriend. I had asked her to join me in Lima, but she did not want to be any part of my "bourgeois awakening." "If I were you, I would not have left the bar on the beach. Based on the life that you have described which although may have been financially hard, also seemed idyllic and carefree. I don't think I would have left Punta Hermosa. I would have preferred an idyllic life to one of consumption and money. You know what I mean - Right?" said Leo.

"Yeah, I do know what you mean, Leo … but for me, it was just like being on holidays, and it was not enough," muttered Kobe.

Kobe then explained how he considered Peru and its women to be extremely exotic and beautiful. For Leo, very little of the country represented beauty, from what he had seen so far. More so, he had to admit that he had seen some beautiful women in the short time he had been there.

"What do you want to eat? Something light or something more substantial?" asked Kobe.

"Something a little hearty and local" replied Leo.

They went to a restaurant named 'La Gloria,' which Kobe and Dom said was considered one of the best in Lima, if not in the world. Kobe tried to reassure Leo that he had been to a lot of different countries, and they would be served some of the finest food there. Leo still felt dizzy, even after all the caffeine. A mix of alcohol, caffeine and the lack of sleep was taking his toll.

Shortly afterwards they arrived at 'La Gloria.' Leo looked around, and the view in the restaurant was incredible. There were so many beautiful women that he was almost left speechless. When they finished their dinner Kobe beat his palms together triumphantly and said. "I love Gloria. The food is amazing." Slapping Dom's back he announced that the time had come for them to head to "Lava," which Kobe assured Leo, was one of the best nightclubs in Lima. They paid the bill and quickly left. As they walked outside the restaurant, the men bumped into some girlfriends of Kobe, who agreed to join them on their jaunt.

As they walked along the streets, the city looked brighter than it had during the drive back to Dom's house. They walked towards the Mira Flores tourist area, which had many with casinos, expensive restaurants and high end hotels. However, the cars that lined the street were old and battered. Although some of the cars looked new, they were not practically expensive, and many had dark tinted windows. The others explained that few wealthy people did not own expensive cars; in order avoid showing off their wealth and making themselves a target. The sidewalk was littered with porters who held colored flags and waved the flags furiously, touting for business and inviting drivers to park next to the sidewalk where they would watch the occupants car for a fee. He noticed that very few people were walking along the pavement. When Leon queried Dom and Kobe about this, they simply replied that "After ten, no one dares to walk around alone in Lima."

After a short walk, they arrived at "Lava." It was a bar in the central part of Mira Flores. The building had a ladder at the side of the premises and through a dark, long corridor; they could hear loud music blaring from the nightclub.

The room was quite dark and full of people. Dom requested a table. As they sat down, it was suddenly filled with drinks and ice from the waiters, and everyone sat on the sofas feeling pleased: Dom, Kobe, Kobe's girlfriends, Leo and Dom's two friends, Giacomo and Diego looking around the group, Dom ordered and opened a bottle of whiskey and made a toast in honor of Leo's arrival and stay.

Following the toast and the emptying of the bottle, Leo got up and asked if anyone else wanted a drink. As he walked through the swarms of people to the bar to order another round of drinks, he realized that, despite the crowding, the room was full of lively people whose eyes smiled as they danced along to the music. Leo did not try to make eye contact with those around him. Instead, he casually looked around to gauge the atmosphere. Leo thought that people back in his country had lost the ability to look at someone directly in the eyes. If it did happen, it tended to arouse suspicion rather than curiosity and friendship.

Among the crazy and wild eyes that danced and smiled to the music around him, Leo was left speechless when he realized that the most beautiful green eyes were staring right at him. Being caught off guard, he did not initially smile back. He stood motionless like a statue transfixed by the woman's gaze until it finally changed direction. He continued to the bar and asked for the drinks in Italian.

Picking up one of the glasses, he saw these same green eyes staring at him in the reflection of the glass. Leo thought that he must have been going crazy. The woman was staring at him, and she smiled seductively tilting her head slightly to the side. Leo took two of the glasses nervously and turned to walk back to the table where his friends were seated.

"What the hell do you want with two glasses?" his cousin asked him.

Leo ignored the question and asked, "Does anyone know who the girl over, there is with the white shirt and black, curly hair?"

The group casually turned to look at the girl, but nobody knew her. His cousin's friend then told him that he knew the girl standing next to her.

"Her friend's name is Jessica. I haven't met the other girl though."

"Well, if you know her friend – it won't take long to get an introduction," Leo said hopefully.

Leo realized that people felt more relaxed and comfortable when they knew someone, especially when they are in an unfamiliar place. Even in a group of people it is always better to know at least someone from that group.

"Hey! Jessica how are you?" Diego asked as he was headed towards the girls closely followed by Leo. The girls looked at ease, as if they expected the men to approach them. Diego walked over and introduced Leo to them who immediately kissed the girls on the cheek, a habit he learned from the Latin Americans earlier that night. The girl with the green eyes introduced herself as Marisol. She explained that her name meant sun and sea in Spanish. Leo invited them both to their table for some initial small talk. The women followed them to the table, and they enjoyed a comfortable and easy conversation. Marisol spoke some English. She studied foreign languages at the University of Lima. She was currently working shifts at a luxury hotel casino.

She had a Dutch and African ancestry. Her father and brothers were professional football players. She was born in Colombia. Leo studied Marisol as she spoke to him. She was twenty-nine years of age, had beautiful dark skin, was tall with black hair that cascaded around her shoulders, and she had the most inviting and mesmerizing green eyes. Her face was symmetrical and exotic, and no feature was excessive. Her lips were gorgeous and full and complimented her features beautifully.

As he looked at her, Leo pleaded internally to God to let him marry her. She was somewhat more delicate than most women, and she did not have the classic Mediterranean features that Leo was usually drawn to. Her shoulders were wonderfully firm, and her back was strong and toned. Leo thought *that the name "Lucky" would be more suitable for her since, only the Greek goddess Tyche "luck" would look so perfect.* She had the most amazing smile, especially when she tilted her head slightly to the side, releasing a light sigh every so often. Her smile was both captivating and seductive.

After a few hours, Dom decided that it was time for them to go. Leo invited Marisol to come with them, but she politely refused. She explained that she had to wake up early to go to work the next day. In a way, Leo felt relieved because he was tired, and the interlude had been quite overwhelming. He had felt a lot of tension, but it was a sweet intensity, and now he felt that he had to rest.

Leo kissed her on the cheek and asked if he could meet up with her the next day. She smiled and said "yes" and walked to the bar to get a piece of paper to write her telephone number on.

The girls left. Leo couldn't believe his luck – he had gone out on his first day in Lima and met the most beautiful woman! He hadn't felt this elated in years.

For the rest of the night, Leo and the rest of the men went to a number of other music clubs in Mira Flores, which were all full of sensual women, keen on meeting dashing young men and looking for love. The women were attractive and friendly. Some were brunettes; others were blonde and some red heads. They were tall with slender physiques, and they had gorgeous smiles as they danced seductively to the music. They were all smiling as though it was their last night on earth, and each looked like they were simply happy. Even though many of the people out did not have much money; Leo noticed that some of the women were sharing their drinks and barely had enough money to get a taxi home at the end of the night; they were still happy and enjoying themselves.

During his stay in Lima, Leo was impressed, by the way, local people enjoyed themselves. Although most people were very simply dressed the fact that they were so confident gave them a very attractive quality. Couples kissed passionately and danced as if they were making love, a seductive combination of stroking and kissing as their bodies melted into each other as they danced. During one evening in Azia, Leo went to a nightclub where he saw couples waiting in a queue for the toilets, desperate for a private space to consummate their passion. In another open-air nightclub, many danced wildly and carefree on the dance floor, under the light rain until the morning hours.

Leo thought that this type of entertainment went beyond the limits of imagination. Most of the men were half-naked, and the women wore broad smiles on their faces. Leo watched with such happiness realizing that these people were experiencing pure euphoria without even having any alcohol. He noticed that many of the women were not reluctant to flirt, and some would reveal their breasts when they wanted their dance partners to give them passionate kisses and stimulate their senses. They danced with complete abandon, endlessly, tirelessly and sensually in such a degree that some couples even looked like they were making love on the dance floor without a care in the world. Their bodies were in rhythm with the music, and it seemed as if they would dance until dawn and then savor the erotic climax in the end. It all resembled a Dionysian ritual.

The next morning was sunny. Leo woke early, and although with a somewhat heavy head from the previous night, he was cheerful and upbeat. He tried to open his eyes. His body felt lightweight, and he smiled when Marisol entered his mind. He felt that this girl was a total mystery. He definitely wanted to see her again. He felt for the first time after a long time that the coming day had some meaning; a purpose. He smiled as he remembered her smile, her lips, her eyes ... he got up and put on his jeans. He found the piece of paper where she had written her phone number. The numbers were clearly written.

He immediately liked her handwriting. He liked the way that women wrote. Their letters always looked somewhat different to the way men wrote. Leo considered it a truly positive sign when a woman gave her home phone number in addition to her cell number. It showed that she was very keen. Leo looked down at the piece of paper. Marisol had only written her home number…

When he came out of the bathroom and went to the living room, Leo found Dom sitting on the couch trying to put on his contact lenses.

"Cousin," he said sleepily to Dom. "What is it? What has changed and made you so refreshed?" Dom replied.

Pretending to ignore his cousin, Leo walked over to the kitchen, opened the fridge door and took out some yoghurt and fruit for breakfast.

"Would you like some yogurt?" he offered.

"Thanks," replied Dom, lying down on the couch while waiting for the tube of yogurt. He was still exhausted. He had clearly drunk too much whiskey the night before.

Leo sensed his cousin's weakened state, so he decided to do some detective work. "So, you have never seen Marisol before?" He began.

"No. I've never seen before. However, I have to admit that she is a very beautiful woman. I would give her a seven out of ten."

Leo was annoyed by the low score Dom gave Marisol, and he instinctively jumped to defend her honor by arguing, "She is exotic, dark and very beautiful. Surely she rates higher than a seven! She also gave me her phone number, and I was hoping to spend the day with her. What do you think?"

"Yes, you should invite her out for some food." Don said enthusiastically.

Shortly after Leo and Dom got dressed and went out in the sun. They went for coffee at "San Antonio" a small cafe in Mira Flores, where his cousin and his friends used to go to have their breakfast of fruit salad and aromatic coffee every morning.

The small cafe was extremely busy. In the morning, it would cater to the office workers before they went to work. The cafe had refrigerators filled with cheese and sausage, and on the rear wall were shelves stacked with different types of bread. In the freezer, there were desserts made from local fruit and ice cream. To the right, there was a dining room with large windows overlooking the road. The floor had black-and-white tiles, but there were white tiles than black. The room had about twenty tables, which were always full. Young women sat there observing the men who entered, smiling and whispering to each other while sipping their coffee. And prevailing over was an aromatic and overpowering smell of scrumptious food ready to satisfy the patrons.

"It is strange but nice," Leo said, "It is curious how men and women don't follow expected patterns of behavior."

"What do you mean?" Dom queried.

"Last night I saw a few women asking men to dance, I saw women standing impatiently outside the toilets to flirt and ask men for their number. Even now women seem to be openly talking about men and smiling at them."

"This is part of our great culture, and it is exactly why we don't want to leave this place," Dom said smiling, sipping his coffee.

The coffee was good, the watermelon juice delicious and the fresh bread heavenly, especially with cheeses and jams.

From there, everyone went to work. That also included Dom, who soon left to go to the restaurant, as he had sorted out some unfinished work before his brother's return later that day. Leo left to call Marisol. He asked her if she would like to join him for a meal that evening. She accepted, and they had had a brief conversation. He liked how her voice sounded on the phone. She seemed so modest; a quality he thought was rare for a woman so beautiful.

During the day, Leo felt strangely pleased. He really wanted to see Marisol again, and he already missed her. He felt strangely awakened, and that love was in the air. *The world was finally, full of possibilities* he thought. He tried to calm himself, and rationalize that it could not be love because they had only just met, on his very first night in Lima, and that it must be from the mere excitement of meeting someone knew. He remembered when he was fourteen-years-old and felt so deeply in love with Avva but in reality, it was not love but infatuation.

"What's the difference?" he thought as he returned to his cousins' restaurant. "What of Rafaela? Was it love? How can you tell a crush from real love?" He was driving himself mad! He desperately wanted to see Marisol. Leo tried to convince himself that he shouldn't be bothered with all these details. He had to empty his head from all his troubled thoughts regarding relationships, love and flings.

Later that morning, Pita, arrived at the restaurant. Leo had not seen him for many years. Leo embraced his cousin saying, "You have put on weight." Pita jovially responded "We eat well here in Peru – but we are always beautiful." And laughed heartily out loud. "I am glad to see that you look strong and healthy" Pita added. They sat down and talked for a very long time. Leo spoke about his family, his new job and the heartache he had experienced with his separation from Rafaela. Pita talked about a number of jobs he was involved in, and that he had been in Brazil, looking at buying a restaurant.

They ate lunch at the restaurant, but Leo said that he wanted to go somewhere else for coffee. So they walked to a nearby place located at Avenue Larco. It was a little cafe that had a few tables inside and out. Leo sat outside at one of the tables with Pita and ordered coffee. He then remarked, "You know what I miss the most from Italy? Having coffee after lunch."

"I would like to go to Sardinia, one day. I have heard it's amazing," replied Pita.

"Unfortunately I haven't been there, but I also hear that it is spectacular."

Pita then began reminiscing about the past. "Can you imagine that while we were building the restaurant, these exact tables were my office? I used to sit here with my pile of papers, small laptop and was constantly talking on the phone" Pita said.

"You weren't distracted by the presence of all these good looking women?" Leo asked laughingly.

"Not so much to be honest. Back then I was really focused on my business" his cousin joked with a wink.

Leo sat back, enjoying the sights of the beautiful women who passed by. These women were spectacular, and he was amazed by their overt sexuality. They were extremely sexy and would wiggle their bottoms under their designer, well-cut skirts. Others wore really tight skinny jeans without any underwear, which left very little to the imagination.

Pita then told Leo a story from his personal experiences about a girl he used to date, Gianna. She was a sexy girl with a beautiful body which sonnets could have been written about. He loved to watch her as she lay face down after making love, gaze at her bottom and delicately caress her body with his hands. Pita said he loved it when Gianna was making the bed; the simple way she would bend and expose her hips was erotic. During his stay in Peru, Leo learned how women maintained their figure and their exquisite bottoms, which were regarded the most prized featured of women in Latin America. It is not just because of their genetics that they have such wonderful bodies but also because of their balanced diet. They mostly steered away from fatty foods and avoided breads and carbs. He noticed that many women were also blessed with skin was smooth and impeccable.

Leo had to agree that women in South America were some of the most beautiful in the world.

After lunch, Leo took a taxi and went back to Dom's apartment to sleep. As he was about to enter the building, he turned to look at the ocean. The ocean was so calm that it reminded him of a morning in the Mediterranean during the middle of June. As he watched the sea, he nostalgically recalled when his father, many years ago would take him almost every Sunday down to the sea. They would sit by the rocks, and his father would take a blue bucket and dive into the deep ocean. He would eventually resurface for air and smile at his son with a bucket full of sea urchins. They would return home where he would proudly empty his catch on the table while his mother looked on. The kitchen would be filled with the aromas of the sea urchins and lemons that they would use the flavor orange flesh from content of the shells. They would slowly eat the sea urchins, laughing and telling stories of past trips when there used to be more sea urchins.

Suddenly, he heard a fluttering behind him. He turned his sweaty head and saw something swiftly pass him by. He felt naked, exposed and terrified. He realized that a small arrow had just passed him. He picked it up. Leo immediately felt dizzy and instead of walking into the apartment, he tried to block and dodge the other advancing arrows, by running across the busy road. After dodging the oncoming traffic, he managed to walk across the road and sit down under a blossoming by the sidewalk. He was panting breathlessly. He felt another dart coming his way. Leo managed to avoid it. He felt like a throbbing gazelle being hunted by a lion. He decided to run back towards the apartment and bumped into the concierge who had been watching Leo's strange movements.

"Did you see something flying in the air?"

"Yes. It is the 'Love Criminal.' He sits here waiting and marks his prey, especially when the weather is nice, and the sun is shining. Two years ago, one morning in May, he killed two students over there," he pointed with his finger to a park bench near the apartment. The concierge spoke quickly and loudly as if he was terrified that he would be attacked next. "Eight years ago, this 'Love Criminal' targeted five thousand arrows in a single day at people in Sourko. He does not care about anyone and shows no mercy. His only occupation is to target innocent people," he said sadly.

Leo said nothing. He was speechless. He did not turn to look at the crime scene. He decided to get home quickly and changed his clothes in a breathless and frightened state. He took off his clothes and threw them on the couch. He hurriedly walked into the bathroom and holding his head; he took a shower. He checked to make sure that all of the windows were closed, as he did not want the perpetrator to get into the apartment and cause further harm. He was scared. After his shower, Leo fell asleep and dreamed that he was walking with his son in a meadow with colorful flowers while leading a white horse by the bridle. His son was holding a flower and asking some questions about the universe. Leo was explaining why the planet Saturn had rings around it and why the dinosaurs had died out.

He felt somewhat more relaxed. The thought of his son always seemed to calm him, and this happy dream of his son in the meadows full of daisies pleased him even more. He smiled as he dreamed happier thoughts.

Leo had been asleep for some time because when he woke it was dark. He entered the living room and found both his cousins sitting on the couch typing on their computers. He asked them how they were, and if they wanted to go out and enjoy the sights of Lima.

"How about we go to a Japanese restaurant tonight?"

"I will call Marisol," said Leo.

"Who is she?" Pita asked as he had not heard her name before.

"It is his dream of Latin America," Dom replied and the men started laughing.

Pita became slightly more serious and said, "Here; women have the ability to wrap you around their little fingers. Listen to me. I will tell you a story that I was once told, and it is the story that I first tell all of my friends who visit Peru. Many years ago, when twenty Serbs moved to Lima to work, their embassy advised them that the one thing that they should fear is the women. Not the high crime rates. Only the women. Everybody laughed loudly and did not take this advice seriously. They were all married man. After six months of living in Peru, they had all found mistresses and divorced their wives.

"Interesting story," said Leo while giving his cousin a strange look. "Why are you telling me this? Don't you think I know? This is all my former wife could think about before we got married. She felt that the marriage would cover up all of her insecurities."

"I agree. I am just warning you. Many women all over the world wish for one thing; marriage. This wish is completely embedded in their minds and trust me, as much as you are aware – just don't forget this! Just be careful and don't be a fool. Some women are cunning, and they will make you think that you are the one and only – the most special man they have ever met. Many men get fooled. It does not mean that you cannot have fun while you're here. Just don't get too attached."

"What? I have no intention of getting married during my vacation! You couldn't possibly think that I was that naïve and stupid?" Leo smiled sarcastically and started to walk into the other room in order to avoid any further discussion.

"You know what I mean. You are vulnerable Leo. Be careful."

Leo became solemn for a little while and responded with "Yes, perhaps you are right. I am vulnerable." He knew all too well that when a man falls in love after heartbreak that he may not be thinking clearly with his dreams driven by excitement and feelings of desire and passion. Love has the power to beat the senses out of the strongest of men. However, when love comes along while a man is feeling at risk, he is consumed a lot easier than if he was not at his most vulnerable and exposed.

Leo reflected on what his cousin had said and realized that it was possible to be lured by the excitement of being in another city, the hope of romance and to get wrapped up by the excitement and the infatuation that comes from meeting someone new.

He perhaps returned to the living room and sat on the couch in a sad state. Pita realized that he had gone too far and that Leo was now skeptical and thinking again about the collapse of his marriage.

"I am not telling you not to enjoy yourself. Just be careful as the delicacies of Lima can also be dangerous!" Pita repeated.

Although it was August, the weather was really warm, so they decided to go out for ice-cream. The weather was extremely foggy despite it not being cold. In Lima, the weather is mostly hazy and the sky grey, but it almost never rains. Despite the haze, the people on the streets were not in a bad mood, in fact; they were mostly all smiling. They walked to the yard of an old mansion, in San Isidro area for their ice-cream. As Leo looked around San Isidro, its streets and shops, it reminded him a little of the *City of Angels* in California.

The Mira Flores and San Isidro were the areas where his cousins and their friends lived. They spent most of their time there, frequently the local casinos, the gym, the best restaurants, night clubs and the movies. Anywhere beyond the boundaries of Mira Flores and San Isidro was another place and existence altogether. It was where they lived. Their lives were hard, living among crime, deprivation, and a general lack of human dignity.

Although it was a beautiful country in parts, Leo realized that Peru was plagued by the three characteristics which affected a lot of Latin America: class inequality, continued political instability and excessive racism. In Peru, the wealth of those with a European ancestry stood out in stark contrast to the Indigenous inhabitants. Although there was a growing mixed race of people as many new immigrants had arrived from the Far East and Africa, there still persisted the century's old racist belief that anyone who was not of European ancestry was inferior. It was an attitude that Leo was uncomfortable with. The class inequality and poverty had resulted in a high crime rate, and it was not just petty crime and burglary. In Lima, there were daily kidnappings. In Mexico or Colombia where the number of abductees who survived, unharmed after a kidnapping in Peru was thankfully quite high.

Despite being a minority in Peru, many of the Europeans amassed great wealth, in stark contrast to other groups. During his subsequent travels, it was a pattern that Leo would see in many other countries.

The big moment was finally here! Leo called Marisol as soon as he got home. She seemed happy to hear from him, and Leo invited her to dine at a restaurant where he was going with his cousins and some friends.

Marisol arrived a little late and when she did make her entrance she had a dazzling smile on her pretty face. They talked about their day; as they ate and drank. Leo watched the mannerisms of Marisol, completely transfixed. He observed how when the waiter brought straws, Marisol took his straw and arranged it nicely into his glass. Leo considered such small details to be important about a person's character and thought that Marisol was very nice and caring.

When Leo's friends decided to go to a casino near Larko Mar, Marisol and Leo went for a walk in the area. Eventually, they reached a secluded waterfront park, called "the park of love." There was a sculpture depicting a man and a woman lying together. The man was over the woman as if they were making love. Leo noticed that she had the expression of a woman in ecstasy, when her lover is inside her. Around the statue was freshly cut lawn and a few swings. The fencing around the park was a low wall covered with colorful mosaics. It was artistically curved and had verses from famous poems. Below each quoted verse was the name of the poet. Leo did not know any of the names, but he liked everything that he read. There was one particular verse that stuck with him:

I have nothing.
Only silence and your mouth.

From where they were stood, Leo could clearly hear the crashing waves of the ocean. It was slightly unfamiliar and a little scary for Leo as he was used to the Mediterranean where the sea was known for singing softly and not scaring people. He walked closer to the wall to view the ocean.

"Have you ever made love on the beach?" Leo asked Marisol.

"Yes," she responded quietly. "It was at night. We were alone."

They looked at each other, and Leo burst out laughing.

"Why are you laughing?" Marisol asked.

"You know why!" He replied.

"No, what?" Marisol replied confused.

"For saying that you were alone," Leo said cheekily.

Marisol laughed nervously feeling slightly uncomfortable.

Leo quickly changed the topic, and soon they were talking about their respective countries. Although Marisol had never really traveled outside of Peru, she had traveled extensively throughout her country.

"Peru is a very beautiful country; there is so much to see outside of Lima. The Andes is magnificent; while the jungle in the north has rare flowers and has fresh, fragrant air, which makes people naturally happy." "Maybe I could stay here forever," said Leo looking at the ocean. "It would be lovely to experience this way of life and to see all of Peru" he continued.

"What stops you?" asked Marisol.

"My son. I have a son who is three years old. He needs my support. He is still young, but I also need him. Maybe when he grows up, I may return here, or I might travel to Brazil. My dream is to own a small bar on the beach in Bahia. I will find the right place; it is safe, and you do not have to be Brazilian to have a good time there. In the evenings, I will drink half of the bar, and then I will make love to the sound of Bossa nova music. In the mornings when I wake up, I will enjoy the sight of the ocean. I will make friends with the local people and become part of the community. The prospect of being able to party on the beaches and the streets, just like the Brazilians do would be exciting. It would be a reposeful lifestyle. In Europe, we aspire to have a relaxing life by working hard – but it is an impossible dream."

Marisol listened to him and smiled. She took his hand in hers. Leo turned and looked at her, smitten by her grace and beauty. "I always smile when I see your smile," and he then leaned over and kissed her for the first time. Her lips were moist and felt wonderful against his lips.

After kissing for a while, Marisol raised her head. "So why Bahia? Why do you want to move to Bahia and not somewhere in the Mediterranean where you would be closer to home?"

Well, before coming here, my brother gave me a disc with music. The first song was Brazilian, and it sounded wonderful, so I figured that Bahia was the place where I would go. I guess I just fantasize about having a different life. I think our sub-conscious can sometimes overpower our psyche and lead us to the unknown. It tells us the truth, and we should not disregard it. So when I hear that song, it allows me to dream what my sub-conscious desires. I believe in the power of the sub-conscious that it often controls our lives. It is where our deepest truth is, and we should not ignore it.

Marisol smiled and titled her head slightly to the side. "I like you so much," she purred and kissed him again encouraging him to let go of his reservations.

"What are you doing tomorrow?" Leo finally asked.

"I work in the morning but in the afternoon and evening, I will be free," Marisol replied.

Like many Latin American women, she was direct when it came to love. When they like someone, they are not coy and don't hide how they feel.

"Well, come to my cousin's apartment. It's at the end of the promenade. We can sit and watch the sunset while enjoying a few drinks. We can share some more of our stories."

"If you have that song about Bahia, then yes," said Marisol smiling.

Leo laughed. "No, but I have some similar ones."

They kissed and started walking towards the main road. Marisol turned and saw the moon. She wondered if there was anything more beautiful or spectacular, so perfectly round and magical. She touched his shoulder, and without saying anything, he turned and looked at her. She then pointed towards the moon like a child showing off something large and wondrous. They remained silent for some time, staring into the sky.

The following day, it was extremely hot, but a cool breeze blew in from the ocean, caressing the sweaty faces of the people who had made a trip to the beach. Marisol came to visit Leo at his cousin's apartment. They kissed before Leo led her to the balcony which had spectacular views of the ocean. They sat themselves upon a bamboo couch, drank Caipirinha and listened to Bossa nova music as they embraced another, relaxing and watching the beautiful sunset. They both wanted to stay in each other's arms forever, wishing that the night would never end.

However, time does not stand still, and as each moment ends. A new one begins. After nightfall, they went inside and made love in Leo's room. Marisol was like a flame that burned in an erotic blaze. The sheets were full of sweat; his body was dripping in her sweat, and his lips were moist from hers. She had passionately kissed and sucked his lips until they went numb. When Leo was inside her, he felt like he could stay there forever. While making love to her, he felt as if the full weight of his body was lost inside her and experienced the same sense of weightlessness as if he was diving in the warm water of the sea. The only thing that kept him anchored to the surface of the Earth was his organ inside his lover. As their lovemaking reached the pinnacle of its climax, Leo could sense the opening of the pores of her delicate skin from which her sweat was poured from, revealing a gentle scent of mint mixed with the salty taste of her sweat. Leo ejaculated on his lover's body. His sperm was salty, and his scent was like the smell of the sea.

Leo thought that the reason for his salty scent was because of his affinity for the sea. He was conceived by the sea. His mother Luna, who was a beautifully tanned blonde with blue eyes, had lived by the beach during her pregnancy and would spend hours every day in the sea. At the time, it was the hottest years in over a century, and thus she had sought the comfort of the sea. After nine months, had come the inevitable pains of childbirth, on a hot noon, on the second Thursday of August, Luna's water broke while she was by the sea. Leo grew up by the beach, happy and carefree. He had an idyllic childhood growing up near the golden sand and beneath a sun that shone almost continuously for ten months a year. The sun tanned his skin and the saltiness of the sea made his hair look constantly unwashed. He grew up happy and for the first twenty years he saw his life through wonderful colors; the green of the sea, the blue of the sky, the golden yellow of sand and the wonderful shades of the skin of the female bodies who bathed at the beach during the summers.

The smells were so strong and beautiful; the scent of the sea in the morning, the coconut aroma of the sunscreen that was applied by people as, they lay in the sun, the aromas of the seafood dishes prepared by the waterfront restaurants in the late afternoon. More so, the most beautiful scents were those from the couples who sat on the beach late at night. They smelt of their perfumes and colognes; rose, lavender, or vanilla.

All those smells and sounds would caress the young Leo as he slept. He always dreamed happy dreams and never had nightmares. He was a very calm child and rarely fretted. Unfortunately, this tranquility was somehow lost during his marriage and after the separation; he thought that the calm that he had once known during his childhood was lost forever.

During the summers of his childhood, he enjoyed playing ball with his friends for hours in the sand, and as he got older, the night-time follies. He recalled with such clarity how he enjoyed many wonderful memories at the beach. He met his first love at fifteen; a blonde, slender girl, her name was Adriana. She was very good-looking and was sixteen-years-old at the time. She came with her parents from the capital for the holidays. It was love at first sight for Leo. Even though he continued to play ball with his friends during the day at the beach, his mind was constantly distracted by the thought of Adriana.

During those days, he spent a lot of time thinking of the girl, who would look at him while he played and give him a beautiful smile whenever he looked over. One evening, Leo finally mustered the courage to approach her. She agreed to go to a beach party that Leo's friends were organizing. He felt happy that he would see her at the party. They smoked and drank beer mixed with icy tequilas that had been bought by the older kids with fake IDs. They later sang by a fire that had been built on the beach. She kissed him back so passionately that she bruised his lips. When they began to make love, Leo was clumsy and somewhat rushed inside her. She was more experienced than him. It would not be the first time that Leo would feel inexperienced when he was with a woman.

At the end of their lovemaking, Leo and Marisol sat in silence for a time with Marisol lying on her stomach and looking at him.

"I think I have fallen for you," she finally said tenderly.

Leo turned and looked at her feeling anxious, his recent emotional pain suddenly feeling raw. His face looked as white as snow, but he remained calm.

"I truly enjoy being with you," he finally said. "I really like you," he continued in a subdued voice. "But I am frightened to fall in love right now as I am still getting over the hurt of my divorce. I am afraid to get too close too soon. I am scared of falling in love and then feeling more pain when I have to leave. I don't know what to do ..."

"Even when you are not vulnerable, love can still knock you down. Trust me on this" Marisol replied gently running her fingers through Leo's hair.

Marisol lowered the tone of her voice and with the reassuring tone as if she was speaking to a scared child "Fear not my 'Leo.' You will feel hurt many times in your life, but your happiness will return when you meet someone new and experience love once again. You will eventually find someone who will suit you, and you will allow yourself to fall in love again. However, you will have to let, go and give her your soul. I can see how you might feel scared now, but when you meet the right woman, she will deserve and need your love without refrain. Just be free, do not rush or push yourself, and you will one day meet the right one."

She left him lying on the bed and rubbing her arms, to keep warm she went to the bathroom. When she came back out, she said. "Be romantic, my dear Leo. You have to tell your woman what bothers you and what you do not like. Women, despite what men might think, are good listeners. You have to be tender with your lover, treat her as an angel. Then you will be able to experience the greatest love. If your lover cannot appreciate you do not get sad. Just move on."

"Do you think it is easy to fall in love with someone and when you realize that they are not the right person, to walk away? I don't." Leo replied thinking of the pain of divorce.

"No. It is not easy. That's why finding love is always a challenge."

Leo handed Marisol a blue sweater so that she would not feel cold. It was nearly dawn, and the temperature had dropped drastically. He kissed her on the forehead and the cheek tenderly and asked, "We are heading to White Beach this weekend. My cousins have a house there. Would you like to come with us? It will be great fun."

"Yes, I have no plans this weekend. We can talk tonight. Give me a call," Marisol replied.

"I cannot see you tonight?" asked Leo, feeling despondent.

"I am working," Marisol said quietly.

He leaned forward and kissed her passionately on the mouth again.

"I really like kissing you. You have such a lovely mouth," he said breathlessly.

Leo then timidly confessed, "I haven't kissed someone for quite some time now. I haven't made love using my body, mind and soul for so long."

Marisol was puzzled after listening to this comment and asked Leo "Do married couples not kiss while making love?"

"Most couples stop being in love long before they realize that they should separate. Sex becomes purely physical and passionless lacking tenderness, intimacy and even kissing. Love becomes a physical need like any other physical need. Then it's just misery, real misery. What was once passionate and intense gradually becomes a life of pathetic mundane routine." Leo explained.

"Who thought marriage could be so perverse" Marisol concluded.

"How can it not be perverse when most people are themselves perverse?" Leo said and embraced her in his arms. Leo remembered how he felt just two days ago, completely done and with no one to embrace. No one knows what will happen from one day to the next. One moment is all it can take to change our lives, which is what makes life so fragile and precious. One moment is enough for good or bad things to happen; the birth of a child, witnessing a terrible accident, the winning goal in a football match, or exchanging smiles with a beautiful woman on the other side of the world. Love is so powerful that it cannot be described. Love is the strongest emotion a person will experience before they die. After the physical act of love-making people tend to feel completely different than they did before. In relative terms, the actual duration of the act of love-making is very short compared with how loving people feel good afterwards. All people who are sensitive will feel closer to their partner after making love, even if they have only recently met. They keep smiling, feeling somehow united. A person's boundaries and inhibitions tend to fall away, and people tend to communicate more openly and cast aside the masks they tend to hide behind their day to day lives.

The next day was Saturday, and the water was surprisingly warm. Dom, Pita and Leo went to Chorillos to pick up Marisol before heading towards White Beach. Leo's cousins claimed that the most beautiful women in Lima resided in Chorillos. Leo did not know if this were true but presumed his cousins were teasing him because of Marisol.

Marisol lived in an apartment with two of her sisters near the best fish restaurant in the area called "Punta Arena." By coincidence, on almost every Sunday afternoon, his cousins could be found enjoying the restaurant's famously delicious crabmeat soup. The "Punta Arena" was an old mansion with an inner courtyard area that was shaded and always felt cool. It had around thirty long tables that sat upon white pea gravel. The men enjoying cold lemonade and Lecce del Tigre, "tiger's milk," a drink made from several spices and fish bones. This place was also famous for a drink called the "blood Panther." It was served in a small glass and made with raw oysters and crushed spices. It was claimed to be an aphrodisiac. Kobe once boasted that he had met a very beautiful and tall woman there, Talia, who had first bought him that drink before they spent hours' afterward making passionate love. Leo was clutching a piece of paper with Marisol's address, but soon spotted Marisol, who was waiting at the front of the building. Leo raised his arm to greet her and walked quickly towards her.

"She is taller than I remembered," said Dom watching Marisol.

"You were so drunk at the time, cousin, that I'm surprised you would have remembered her at all!" Leo replied.

Marisol leaned forward and kissed Leo tenderly and asked if he had time to meet her sisters. He said "yes" and turning to his cousins nodded that he would return shortly. Leo then went into the small run down building. The walls were filled with holes, and there were patches of unpainted cement. The stairs were wooden, and there was no elevator. Climbing the stairwell, Leo could hear deafening noises coming from the apartments; bickering couples, crying babies, and loud vibrating salsa music.

Finally, they reached Marisol's apartment. After knocking at the door, a very tall, striking woman with curly hair, whose hair was tied up, answered the door. She smiled the same wide smile which reminded Leo of Marisol. This woman was introduced to Leo as Marisol's older sister. Sitting across the door, on an old couch covered with green cloth and worn wooden arms was Marisol's other sister. She was just as beautiful and was cradling an infant that she was feeding. The two girls wore jeans, had similar but different colored shirts and sandals.

The three sisters were smiling constantly, and they almost looked identical. They had some differences, but it was clear that these women were siblings. The girl sitting on the sofa, Alicia, could speak some broken English, and the girl who opened the front door, Elizabeth, could only speak Spanish.

Leo felt very welcome in their home, although they could not communicate clearly. Alicia was the most talkative of the women and kept kissing the baby whom she introduced as Alonso. Leo assumed that baby Alonso was the result of a relationship that ended right after Alicia announced that she was pregnant. It was all too common occurrence in Peru for a woman to fall pregnant, and for the father to not only refuse to marry, but to completely disappear once they find out about the pregnant. Most of these women, due to their religious convictions, will choose to keep the child and raise the child on her own, with the help of family. Marisol acted as a translator as Alicia asked Leo if he liked the warm weather in Peru and what he thought of their country.

Leo replied that he really liked the weather. He looked around the room and noticed that the white walls were almost completely filled with cracks. These were many family photos, and on the table, there was a photo of three farmers in a green meadow with three baskets of colorful flowers. The apartment had its own smell that came from the stale, threadbare Persian carpet. It had a musty odor. The women offered their guest a cold drink, which he hurriedly drank, remembering that his cousins were still waiting outside. Leo then got up quickly from his chair, said good-bye to the sisters with a kiss on the cheek and patted the baby before taking Marisol's hand and hastily leaving the apartment.

Pita and Dom were waiting patiently outside, speaking on their mobile phones when the couple reached the car. The men were engrossed in their own conversations. Eventually, they finished their calls and began driving south towards Punta Hermosa. They then drove towards Azia before heading to White beach.

From the highway, they could see the hills on one side and the beautiful beaches on the other. For the most part, both seemed deserted. Occasionally, they saw small houses and dusty villages in the middle of nowhere and little taverns that were shattered and closed. As they drove further away from Lima, the climate changed. The mist gave way revealing the sky of mesmerizing blue; the only color that broke the shimmering light of the sun.

The trip was turning out to be wonderful. During their drive, Leo would turn to look at Marisol, who would be looking out towards the sea. She was wearing sunglasses. *How amazing this beautiful woman is,* he would tell himself. Occasionally, she would turn and catch him staring at her. She would instantly break into that smile of hers without having to say a word. Leo knew that memory of her watching and smiling at him, would be in his mind and haunt him for a long time afterwards.

The House in White Beach

There are some places on Earth that were created by God when he was in a good mood, Leo thought. Leo thought that White Beach must have been one of those places. Simply put, it was 'God's own country,' located some ninety-six kilometers south of Lima.

The sand was fine and shimmered white in the light. It did not stick to the body. Leo took a handful of the warm sand and observed its simple beauty. He thought that it was completely unique as he let it run through his fingertips transfixed by the shades of white and gold grains, mixed with small pebbles and shells. It was called White Beach because of the color of the sand that stretched out along the coast for four kilometers.

There was a little house built near the beach, which was white with blue doors. It had a few paintings of the Ancient Greek God Poseidon on the external walls. Inside there was an open courtyard with a small pool and a table with six chairs. It had one door and four walls. The door always remained open, since it could not be forced shut as much as the local residents tried in vain.

The wind was blowing when they arrived. The odors were alluring and carried the scent of mangoes from the south, love fragrances from the north, peppermint aromas from the west, and the unique scent of the sea from the east. According to folklore, during the nights of February, the sea washed up a lot of colorful fish that would not die on the sand, but fly around the local houses instead. The house was full of love. It was as if love was a permanent resident. Leo left his bag on the floor and browsed through the house for a while. It was very bright. There was a wooden table with a colorful tablecloth that resembled the fabric that covered sofas. Passing between the couches, he went out on one of the ground-level terraces, where there was another large sofa and a smaller table. The terrace had a white ceramic finish and next to it; there was a small square of grass. He looked out at the beach where the sand complimented the beautiful blue ocean.

Although Leo's visit to White Beach was supposed to be just for two days, he ended up staying for eight days. Although his cousins and their friends rented the house year round they would only spend four months there; from December to late March. Long after leaving Peru, Leo would remember the time at White Beach and feel as if he had never left. It was very much a paradise. During their stay, they ate fish, Argentinean beef and drank Pisco on the terrace. Leo felt relaxed in his surroundings and enjoyed the wonderful company. His cousins and friends made him feel comfortable from day one. He was glad to have reconnected with his cousins and to have met their friends, Kobe, Kily, Zamora and his wife, as well as "crazy" Herman with his lover Flora.

Herman was the best roaster, and he would cook for hours on end with enormous enthusiasm and skill. During one of the many feasts that was put on where the cooking time would take at least ten hours, Herman passed the time by telling jokes about his hometown Monterrey. Herman would cook naked from the waist up, wearing a faded blue hat and often with a Cuban cigar hanging out of the corner of his mouth. Every now and then, he would pause his cooking in order to take some photos. Herman was the soul of the party. His positive disposition was infectious, and he could persuade his friends to have a party any time of day, irresponsible of how they felt. In the heat of one really hot afternoon, Marisol and Leo showered together. As the water fell from the shower Marisol closed her eyes and raised her head to one side to feel the cold water on her face. Leo watched as the water cascaded over her taut body. He appreciated her body, and he enjoyed looking at her breasts and how her nipples hardened when the cold water ran across them. He loved her sweet face and full lips, which constantly reminded him of the unbridled passion they frequently shared together.

There was a wooden window over the bathroom, and Leo reached his hand to open it. The sun's rays burned violently while the wind carried the fragrance of the sea mixed with the fragrance of love. It was as if butterflies, seahorses and hundreds of white and yellow, small daisy petals had entered the room *this particular sense of love is regretfully missing from my country;* Leo sadly thought.

They caressed each other's bodies as they dressed and went out. It was already evening, and Marisol was wearing jean shorts and a white shirt. Leo was wearing white linen pants, and a shirt. He had combed his hair back and tied a small silver lion around his neck. Marisol noticed that her lover had failed to put on underwear. When she queried him about this, Leo replied that he "never wore any underwear." He explained that because he grew up by the beach, he was almost always going in and out of the water and would, therefore, not wear underwear. This had become a habit to the point that he did not feel comfortable when he wore it. "Do you feel more comfortable like this?" Marisol teased, reaching out towards his manhood and feeling aroused by what she felt. Leo felt aroused by Marisol's seductive touch and smiled. "I think you can feel the answer for yourself!"

They climbed to the rooftop terrace and opened a bottle of Pisco, cut some mango and lay on the couch watching the sea. "Have you been here before Marisol?" asked Leo. "I have traveled along the road going south once, but I have never been here nor have I experienced this beautiful beach before. I must admit that it is perfect here" she replied.

"On the island where I grew up, there are beautiful beaches, but they are usually small and crowded. We do not have secluded, private beaches. After reminiscing about his childhood home for a while, Leo took Marisol by the hand who was feeling tipsy, down to the beach. As Leo removed his shoes, his lover started to dance seductively but playfully to the Latin music that was blaring from the house. Leo watched her sweet moves, and when she stopped he scooped her into his arms, laughing loudly. He kissed her wildly and passionately and told her how he wanted to take her lips away with him. Marisol stroked him tenderly while looking deeply into his eyes.

Leo and Marisol had become soulful lovers and as lovers, it was hard for lovers not to experience living in the moment. They both realized that their time together was finite. Leo's stomach churned, his mouth was dry, and his chest was heavy whenever he thought about it. And yet it was strangely different feeling from what he had felt when he had first started his journey back in Amsterdam. He felt a burden, but it was different. It had to do with caring and not love loss. While lying awake at night, with Marisol slept tucked up against him, Leo would reflect on these feelings. There are those couples that simply match. When you see them together, you feel that they are suited like a pair of gloves without even knowing anything about them. They exude a sense of serenity in each other's presence; you can feel and see their devotion and love towards each other. You feel that they will be always be inseparable – that they will grow old together and that their love will endure the test of time. But for couples like Marisol and Leo, their love story is dictated by circumstances where they know that the love that they are feeling has to be fleeting, and even though they may perfectly fit, they do not have the luxury of time.

Leo made sure to spend as much time as he could with Marisol and make the most of those precious hours together. He cherished their time together, and their lovemaking had become even more sensual and erotic. Over the next three weekends, Leo and Marisol would go to White Beach and spend every moment together, just the two of them, making love with wild abandon.

They would visit the town centre and dance at the local club until the early hours of the morning. They would return quite tipsy to that wonderful house at White Beach. They would make love at the same spot on the beach where the waves would break and caress them up to their knees. Waking up late, Marisol and Leo would spend the morning basking in the sun. When noon arrived, they would make love again and fall asleep in each other's arms despite their sweaty disposition.

Leo would awake in the afternoon feeling the scented sea breeze coming in from the open window and to the sound of Marisol speaking softly and sweetly. He loved her sweet voice and felt connected to it. Marisol had a natural gift of calming everything around her when she spoke. Her voice was lyrical and light, yet at the same time it was calm and stable. It felt reassuring and soothed away the pain of any thoughts Leo had when he thought about the time which grew ever closer of when he would have to leave. During the afternoons, they walked on the beach and sang softly. They would cajole each other as they walked. They would kiss often, fervently. They both knew how important kissing was in the act of love since without it lovemaking was incomplete.

They joked and talked about the similarities and differences between their countries. Their time with each other was perfect, and they both wished that their weekends together could last for years.

Leo could not help but smile when he saw Marisol. She was a beautiful woman whom he enjoyed spending time with. Marisol seemed gentle and true, and she was not afraid to confess how she felt about him. It was such a contrast to his past relationships where he felt his ex-wife and previous lovers would ration out their feelings and emotions as if always keeping something back. However, Marisol was different.

During their final evening together at the house on the White Beach, they sat on the roof terrace looking out at the full moon over sitting the calm ocean. A band of reflected moonlight ran across the ocean near the shore. It reminded Leo of the myth of the "Moonpath." "Look at the Moonpath," he said absently.

"What's that?" Marisol asked, lifting her head from his shoulder and looking up towards him. Leo looked down tenderly towards his lover, gently stroked his lips across hers before continuing.

"It is that path of light that you can see reflected off the water. According to folklore, if a couple makes love within the Moonpath, the moon will impart its magical properties, and the souls of the couple will stay together eternally."

Marisol stared tenderly into Leo's eyes for a moment, and without saying a word, stood up and taking his hand, led him down to the beach. Letting go of Leo's hand, she walked towards the sea, removed her clothes and waded out into the water. Once she was in the middle of the Moonpath, she turned back towards Leo beckoning. Taking his cue, Leo followed Marisol's lead. As he met her in the light of the moon, he swept her into his arms as she wrapped her legs around his waist, and they hungrily kissed, their love as intense, perfect, romantic and transient as the moment and setting around them.

The next morning, Leo, awoke and saw Marisol already dressed. She was tying her hair up oblivious to the Leo, whom she thought was still asleep. He was completely captivated by her beauty even as she did such a simple task. She silently left the room. Leo got up and watched from the window as she walked down to the beach. The ocean was a dark green; the clouds were overcast and heavy with rain. The sand was dull as Marisol sat upon it and looked towards the ocean. Leo quickly dressed and followed her down.

As Leo approached, Marisol turned around, shouted and stood up. Her face was wet from tears. Leo took her in his arms. "Even if I never see you again, I have never felt so much passion, such love, such awakening. It is as if I have been rejuvenated, refreshed and every time you smile – it radiates my soul." Leo said as Marisol buried her face in his chest. When he had finished, speaking she arched her back and lifted her face towards him. Rain began to fall.

It was a sign from heaven, and Leo immediately looked up. Marisol began to laugh loudly and nervously as the rain became heavier. They stretched out their hands and opened their mouths, tilting back their heads to allow the raindrops to fall into their mouths.

"So you will smile every time you think of me?" Marisol asked her beautiful smile having returned. She really liked this idea and kissed him while smiling. As the cold breeze began to blow across White Beach, they quickly ran back towards the house.

Over the next few days after they had returned to Lima, Leo saw Marisol for a few hours every day after she finished work. She either came to his cousin's apartment, or they would meet at the "Larco Mar" and enjoy long walks together. They were becoming very good friends as well as lovers, and they felt as if they were now something more – soul mates.

One afternoon while they were sitting on Dom's balcony, Leo decided to create a new drink and name it "White Beach" to commemorate their time together. He filled a short glass with ice cubes and sliced strawberries before adding his secret ingredient of "Marisol perfume" – mango rum.

Once the sun had set, but before it got dark, Leo made love to Marisol on the chair. When they finished, they sat hugging and staring at the ocean. They remained there and watched the ocean until the early hours of the morning. It was the last time that they would make love.

On the day of his flight, Leo called Marisol so that they could arrange to meet in the afternoon at Larco Mar, after Marisol got off work. Leo, having been held up by traffic, arrived slightly late and when he arrived, could see her standing alone fearing that she had missed him and that they would not see each other one last time.

He stood for a while, watching her feeling the impending sadness of never seeing her again wash over him before he finally approached her.

They walked around the Larco Mar area. After a while, Marisol suddenly forced Leo against a small wall. They embraced, and Leo leaned forward to hungrily taste her lips one final time.

Marisol then fumbled in her bag and gave Leo a parting gift - a small silver Inca God to wear around his neck. Leo looked at her and said, "I'll call, and I'll send you emails, and I'll be back to see you. Please come and visit me. You can always stay with me for as long as you want."

She looked at him miserably and said, "It will be difficult because I have to work and can't take time off. But maybe, one day. We had such a lovely time together. I wish the best for your son." And she leaned forward and kissed him quickly on the lips.

"I can't wait to see you again," Leo said wishing that he could believe that they would see each other another time.

They finally walked towards the taxi rank. Leo watched, as Marisol got into the taxi and then within minutes; the car had disappeared from sight. He had the most awful feeling in the pit of his stomach, as he knew that they had made a rare connection. At that moment, he realized that once again he was going to endure the pain of separation, but it would be worse than previously as the separation of two people who were harmonically joined together, where the interruption of this harmony would upset the soul and leave behind an everlasting void.

He put his hands in the pockets of his pants and started to walk toward his cousin's nearby restaurant. As he walked he gently kicked the stones on the pavement, reflecting on his entire trip. He felt like a lost child as his mind was filled with random thoughts, memories and inexplicable feelings.

Despite the fervent hopes, he had expressed to Marisol before she had left, he realized that he had probably lost his Marisol forever, which made him feel very sad and lonely. On the other hand, he was also aware that he felt rejuvenated by their special connection and that he had once again found the desire to live. More importantly, he found himself again. Despite his current sadness, Leo felt calm, erotic, cheerful, and happy as he realized how much he had enjoyed traveling, reconnecting with the sea and making some wonderful friends.

He recalled how after his separation with Rafaela, he would return home to an empty house. He would turn on the TV and watch something, even if it was silly with nonsense dialogues and to dull, his sense of loneliness. He realized that the people in his life had become increasingly distant, and was so miserable and depressed that he believed that everybody thought he was boring and avoided his company.

He recalled how sad he had felt at his divorce, as it would mean that he would no longer live with his son, and he would have to start a new life. He had started his journey at a complete loss and with so much angst and yet in a matter of weeks his life had changed dramatically and drastically.

At the start of this journey, he had thought that he was lost forever but now everything had changed. His interlude and connection with Marisol had brought him back to life, and he felt that he could live again. He felt awakened, and that there was no turning back. Everything was new again. He felt like when his son was born, and he had heard him crying for the first time, sitting outside the delivery room. There was a mixture of excitement and nervousness. He concluded that Marisol was his rebirth; she taught him how to face the future with a new- found sense of optimism.

Despite the fact, he would never see her or Peru again; Leo would always remember her and how she had saved him when he was at his most dire. He had hit rock bottom and was in the depths of depression. However, Marisol had taught him how to love, and gave him the will to live. She opened herself to him unconditionally. He had expressed himself to her in an open and honest way that he had never thought possible. She taught him that he did not need to fear love and that he could submit his soul again. Not just for sex, but to be truly intimate with someone again. She had rekindled Leo's fate that he would meet someone else one day who he would be able to share the rest of his life with. As he flew back home, Leo continued to play the events of his trip over in his mind. He thought about the start of his trip. He was broken and lonely, destroyed by the end of his marriage. However, thanks to a chance meeting with a beautiful and exotic woman, his senses had been awakened, and he had been brought back to life. And suddenly everything seemed new. It was like he had woken up from a dream, and his life had a different meaning. He felt reborn.

The weight inside him that had disturbed him so much at the start of the trip had gone. The loss of Marisol from his life had saddened him, but it did not bring with him a sense of hopelessness because he now knew that he had the courage to start again. He had developed a weapon that could repel that feeling. It was a weapon made from the love of Bossa nova; from the sun; from the sea; the sand and the kindness of one-woman – Marisol. He felt calm again like when he was a child by the seaside.

Unconsciously he turned his head to the left. Two seats in front of him sat a young blond woman with piercing blue eyes. She had a tanned face and looked as if she was a Northern European tourist who had just finished her holidays and was returning to Europe. She was typing on a small computer which occasionally beeped as she softly typed upon the keyboard.

Leo stared at her for a while. After some time, she turned her eyes and looked directly at him. He returned her gaze and smiled warmly at her. "Good morning. Is the noise from the keyboard bothering you?" she asked.

"Good morning, my name is Leo. No, it is not bothering me at all."

She returned Leo's smile, "I'm Monica," she said.

"From Sweden?" Leo queried.

"No, Switzerland!"

"What would a Swiss be doing in Peru? Holidaying in Cusco?" Leo asked.

"No, I came to see my boyfriend," she replied matter-of-factly.

Leo smiled and looked out the window. Although the pain of leaving Marisol was still very raw, as he drifted off to sleep, a lingering smile could, nevertheless, be seen on his face, as he thought of her, and the evergreen, perfect memory of the time that they had spent together. With the weight of hopelessness finally lifted from his chest, Leo could once again dream in peace – and dream of finding love.

Wattle Publishing

Wattle Publishing is an independent publishing house based in London. We publish fiction and non-fiction works in a range of categories.

'Join us' on Twitter: @wattlepub
'Like us' on Facebook: Wattle Publishing
www.wattlepublishing.com